# I, R(

SH

Real life scier saac Asimov wrote thes st 194? - when most people just laughed at a of robots doing many of the jobs done by human beings. But today, we have robots. They do many skilled jobs in factories, and do them better than poor, weak, unreliable human beings. Our robots don't look like human beings, of course, and they can't think, or reason, or make decisions. But in Asimov's world . . .

Dr Susan Calvin is a robot psychologist. She remembers the long history of robot development, and some of the problems that Greg Powell and Mike Donovan had to deal with. They were an experienced team of robot engineers, used to the blazing heat of the planet Mercury, and the freezing temperatures of the asteroid stations. Used to robots which were stronger, more efficient, and almost cleverer than they were.

OXFORD BOOKWORMS LIBRARY

*Fantasy & Horror*

# I, Robot

SHORT STORIES

Stage 5 (1800 headwords)

Series Editor: Jennifer Bassett
Founder Editor: Tricia Hedge
Activities Editors: Jennifer Bassett and Alison Baxter

ISAAC ASIMOV

# I, Robot

## SHORT STORIES

*Retold by*
Rowena Akinyemi

OXFORD UNIVERSITY PRESS

# OXFORD

UNIVERSITY PRESS

Great Clarendon Street, Oxford OX2 6DP

Oxford University Press is a department of the University of Oxford.
It furthers the University's objective of excellence in research, scholarship,
and education by publishing worldwide in

Oxford New York

Auckland Cape Town Dar es Salaam Hong Kong Karachi
Kuala Lumpur Madrid Melbourne Mexico City Nairobi
New Delhi Shanghai Taipei Toronto

With offices in

Argentina Austria Brazil Chile Czech Republic France Greece
Guatemala Hungary Italy Japan Poland Portugal Singapore
South Korea Switzerland Thailand Turkey Ukraine Vietnam

OXFORD and OXFORD ENGLISH are registered trade marks of
Oxford University Press in the UK and in certain other countries

ISBN 978 0 19 479228 8

Typeset by Wyvern Typesetting Ltd

Printed in Hong Kong

*Illustrated by*: Richard Bennett

Word count (main text): 22,500 words

For more information on the Oxford Bookworms Library,
visit www.oup.com/bookworms

# CONTENTS

# The Three Laws of Robotics

1 A robot must not injure a human being, or allow a human being to come to harm.
2 A robot must obey the orders given by human beings unless they conflict with the First Law.
3 A robot must protect itself as long as such protection does not conflict with the First or Second Laws.

Book of Robotics, 56th Edition, 2058 A.D.

# DR SUSAN CALVIN

I looked at my notes and I didn't like them. I'd spent three days at the United States Robots Company, its offices and factories like a small city, and I needed more personal information for my newspaper. And so I went to interview Dr Calvin.

Susan Calvin had been born in the year 1982. At the age of twenty she had met Dr Alfred Lanning of US Robots who had shown her the first robot with a voice. It was a large, clumsy, ugly robot which was going to be sent to the mines on Mercury.

Susan was a cold girl, plain and colourless, who disliked the world around her. But as she watched and listened to the robot, she felt the beginning of a cold excitement. In 2008 she completed her final degree at Columbia University, and began work at US Robots as the first robot psychologist.

For fifty years she watched the development of robots – and now she was leaving US Robots at the age of seventy-five.

'My newspaper reaches the whole solar system,' I said to Dr Calvin. 'We have three billion readers, Dr Calvin. They would like to hear your views on robots.'

Dr Calvin didn't smile at me. I don't think she ever smiled. She was small and thin and her eyes were sharp, though not angry.

'How old are you?' she wanted to know.

'Thirty-two,' I said.

'Then you don't remember a world without robots,' Dr Calvin began. 'There was a time when human beings faced the world alone and without a friend. Now we have robots to help us – stronger, more useful, more capable than we are. Human beings are no longer alone. Have you ever thought of it that way?'

*'Then you don't remember a world without robots'*

4

'I'm afraid I haven't.'

'To you, a robot is a robot. Made by humans and, if necessary, destroyed by humans. But you haven't worked with them, so you don't know them. They're cleaner, better creatures than we are. In the beginning, of course, robots couldn't talk. Afterwards, they became more human. But it took US Robots a long time. The first robots sent out to Mercury failed. If you want to know about the second expedition, young man, I advise you to visit Gregory Powell. He's still living in New York – he's a grandfather now. But in those days he and Michael Donovan were the engineers who were given our most difficult cases.'

'I can visit Mr Powell later,' I agreed. 'But please tell me what you remember now.'

She spread her thin hands on her desk and looked at them. 'There are two or three of their cases that I know about,' she said.

'Start with Mercury,' I suggested.

'Well, I think that the Second Mercury Expedition was sent out in 2015. It consisted of two engineers – Gregory Powell and Michael Donovan – and a new robot, the SPD robot . . .'

# RUNAROUND

Mike Donovan, his red hair wild, rushed down the stairs towards Greg Powell. 'What have you been doing in the sublevels all day?' he asked feverishly. He paused. 'Speedy hasn't come back.'

Greg Powell stopped on the stairs. 'You sent him after the selenium?'

'Yes.'

'And how long has he been outside?'

'Five hours now.'

Silence. What a situation! Here they were, on Mercury exactly twelve hours, and already in the worst sort of trouble.

They went up the stairs and into the radio room, untouched for ten years. The equipment was out of date and the room looked depressing.

Powell said, 'Start at the beginning, Mike, and let's get this straight.'

'I tried to speak to him by radio, but radio isn't any good on the Mercury Sunside. That's one of the reasons the First Expedition failed. I followed his position for two hours – look at the map.'

Donovan threw the map on to the table. 'The red cross is the selenium pool – thirty kilometres away. The blue crosses show Speedy's position.'

For the first time Powell looked worried. 'Are you serious? This is impossible.'

'There it is,' said Donovan.

The blue crosses made a circle around the red cross of the selenium pool. Powell's fingers touched his brown moustache, a sign of his anxiety.

'In the two hours I watched him,' Donovan added, 'he went round that pool four times. He seems likely to continue for ever. Do you realize the position we're in, Greg?'

Powell said nothing. Oh, yes, he realized the situation they were in. The photocell banks in the walls and roof, which alone protected them from the full heat of Mercury's terrible sun, were badly damaged. The only thing that could save them was selenium. The only thing that could get the selenium was Speedy. If Speedy didn't come back, there would be no selenium. No selenium, no photocell banks. No photocell banks – well, death by slow boiling is not a pleasant way to die.

Donovan rubbed his red hair and spoke bitterly. 'How can everything have gone wrong so soon? The great team of Powell and Donovan sent to Mercury to repair the Sunside Station. A routine job. And we fail on the first day. We'll be in trouble for this.'

'We'll be in worse trouble here,' said Powell quietly, 'if we don't do something quickly.'

'Well, what are we going to do?' Donovan looked at Powell eagerly. 'Come on, Greg. You've got an idea, haven't you?'

'We can't go after Speedy ourselves, Mike – not on the

Sunside. Even if we wear the new insosuits, they won't protect us for more than twenty minutes in direct sunlight. But we've got six robots down in the sublevels. Maybe we can use them, if they still work.'

There was sudden hope in Donovan's eyes. 'Are you sure? Six robots from the First Expedition? But that was ten years ago.'

'Well, they've got positronic brains – very simple ones, of course.' He put the map in his pocket. 'Let's go down.'

*

The robots were on the lowest sublevel. All six of them were extremely large, over three metres tall.

Donovan whistled. 'Look at them! The chests must be three metres around.'

'Old machinery,' Powell explained. 'I've examined them – they may talk.'

Powell took an atomic battery from his pocket and put it into the chest of one of the robots. 'You! Do you hear me?'

The robot's head bent slowly and the eyes looked at Powell. 'Yes, Master!' Its voice sounded rusty and tired.

'Can you go outside? In the light?'

The robot's brain worked slowly. 'Yes, Master.'

'We will take you upstairs and outside the station. You will go about thirty kilometres and you will find another robot, smaller than yourself. You will order him to return. If he doesn't wish to return, you must bring him back by force.'

'Yes, Master.'

'All right. Follow me.'

The robot didn't move. 'I cannot. You must ride me.'

Powell stared and pulled his moustache. 'An old robot . . . Of course! He can't move without human control. Someone has to ride him like a horse. What do we do now?'

'We can't go thirty kilometres outside, with a robot or without,' Donovan said. 'Wait a minute. Give me that map! This is a mining station. What's wrong with using the tunnels?'

Donovan studied the map. The mining station was a black circle, and black lines showing the tunnels stretched out from it. 'Look, we can come out here, at exit 13A, five kilometres from the selenium pool.'

'Right. Get your insosuit,' Powell said.

It was the first time they had worn the insosuits. They were light, but big and ugly. A human being wearing an insosuit could survive the sun on Mercury for twenty minutes.

'Are you ready to take us to exit 13A?' Powell asked the robot.

'Yes, Master.'

Powell climbed up on to one robot and Donovan got up on another. There were seats on the backs of the robots, and two long ears to hold on to. The two huge robots moved through the door and along a narrow passage into the tunnel. They moved slowly, at a speed that never varied: they were unable to hurry.

After a time, they came to the end of the tunnel and they went up some stairs to a tiny substation, empty, airless. A tall cliff of black rock cut off the sunlight, and the deep night shadow of an airless world enclosed them. Before them, the shadow of the cliff reached out and ended suddenly in a hard

*They moved slowly, at a speed that never varied.*

line, before the blinding white light of Mercury Sunside.

Donovan looked at the instruments on his wrist. 'The temperature is eighty centigrade!' He stared out over the broken, rocky ground. 'See anything?'

'There's a dark area over there that may be the selenium pool. But I don't see Speedy.'

Donovan stood up on his robot's shoulders. 'I think . . . Yes, there he is. He's coming this way!'

'I see him!' shouted Powell. 'Let's go!'

The robots began to move.

'Faster!' shouted Donovan.

'No use!' cried Powell. 'These robots can move at only one speed.'

They moved out from the shadow of the cliff, and the sunlight poured down white-hot around them.

'Keep your eyes on Speedy, Mike,' Powell said. 'It's going to get hotter.'

Robot SPD-13 ran easily across the broken ground. SPD robots were the fastest robots produced by the United States Robots Company. They were built for the low gravity, the fierce temperatures and the broken ground of Mercury.

'Speedy!' shouted Powell into his radio. 'Come here!'

Speedy looked up and saw them. He stopped suddenly and remained standing for a moment. Then he turned and ran away, kicking up dust behind him. Over their radios, Donovan and Powell heard him singing a song.

Donovan said weakly, 'Greg, he's crazy.'

'He's not crazy,' Powell said. 'A robot's only a robot. There's something wrong with him that's confusing his brain patterns. Once we find out what it is, then we can fix it.'

The two men went back to the shadow of the cliff and got down from their robots.

'What did you say to Speedy when you sent him for the selenium?' Powell asked. 'Did you tell him that it was urgent? Important?'

'No,' Donovan replied. 'It was just a routine order. I just told him that we needed some selenium and that he should go and get it.'

'Right,' said Powell. 'Well, let's start with the Three Laws of Robotics that are built into a robot's positronic brain. First, a robot must not injure a human being, or allow a human being to come to harm. Second, a robot must obey the orders given by human beings unless they conflict with the First Law. Third, a robot must protect itself, unless this conflicts with the First or Second Laws.'

'And how does that help us?'

'Speedy is one of the most expensive robots available. To protect the SPDs, their brains were made a little differently: the Third Law was built in more strongly than is usually done. Perhaps there's a danger at the selenium pool which Speedy is avoiding.'

'What danger?'

'Well, where does the selenium come from?'

'It's produced after a volcano has been active,' Donovan said quickly.

'That's it! Maybe there's some gas above the selenium pool, escaped from underground, which is a risk to Speedy. Perhaps carbon monoxide. At this temperature, it could combine with the iron parts of Speedy's machinery and cause him to explode.'

Donovan nodded. 'The Third Law drives him back from the pool, and then when he gets away from the pool, the Second Law drives him forward towards the pool again. And unless we can find a way to stop him, he'll go on doing that – giving us the runaround!'

There was silence. They had to think fast!

'There's always the First Law,' Powell said at last.

Donovan looked up.

'We're desperate,' Powell said. 'A robot can't watch a human being in danger without helping. I'm going out there now to see what the First Law will do.'

'Wait, Greg!' Donovan protested. 'You can't go out there into the sun just like that. We must choose which of us . . .'

But Powell, on his robot, was off into the sunlight. The old robot moved slowly towards Speedy, who was near the selenium pool. It seemed a long way. When Powell was three hundred metres away, he got down from the old robot and continued on foot. He felt the heat of the rocks through the boots of his insosuit, and he moved with difficulty because of the low gravity. He looked over his shoulder once at the blackness of the cliff's shadow and realized that he had come too far to return now. More than ten minutes had passed!

'Speedy!' Powell called anxiously into his radio, when he got near enough. 'I must get back to the shadow or the sun will kill me. It's life or death, Speedy. I need you.'

Speedy stopped, but did not turn. Powell saw a movement out of the corner of his eye.

'Master, you are in danger,' a slow voice said.

Powell turned quickly and stared in surprise at the huge old robot moving towards him.

'I must not move without a Master on me, but you are in danger.'

Of course! The First Law came before everything else. But Powell didn't want the old robot: he wanted Speedy. 'Stay away!' he shouted urgently at the old robot. 'I order you to stay away!'

It was quite useless: you could not beat the First Law. The robot said stupidly, 'You are in danger, Master.'

Powell looked about him desperately. The sun was burning through his insosuit and he was breathing with difficulty. The ground all around him seemed to move in the heat; he couldn't see clearly.

He called again, desperately, 'Speedy! I'm dying! Speedy, I need you!'

Suddenly, he felt metal fingers on his arm and heard a worried, metallic voice in his ears. 'Boss, what are you doing here? And what am I doing? I'm so confused —'

'Never mind,' Powell whispered weakly. 'Get me into the shadow of the cliff – and hurry!'

\*

Powell woke to see Donovan bending over him and smiling anxiously. 'How are you, Greg?'

'Fine! Where's Speedy?'

'Right here,' Donovan said. 'I sent him out to one of the other selenium pools. This time I explained that it was essential to get that selenium urgently. He got it back in forty-two minutes. He's still apologizing for the runaround he gave us.'

Powell put out his hand and held Speedy's metal fingers for a moment. 'It's OK, Speedy.' Then he rubbed his face.

*Suddenly, he felt metal fingers on his arm.*

The air was beautifully cool! 'You know, Mike, when we finish here, they're going to send us to one of the space stations —'

'No!'

'Yes! That's what Dr Calvin told me. I was going to fight the idea. But it's all right with me now. 273 centigrade below zero. Won't it be pleasant?'

# REASON

Half a year later, the boys had changed their opinion. The flame of a huge sun had been changed for the cold blackness of space. But although the background had changed, Powell and Donovan were again faced with a positronic brain which did not work properly. They discovered that soon after they arrived at the Station.

Gregory Powell spoke slowly. 'One week ago, Donovan and I made you.' He frowned as he stared at Robot QT-1, and pulled his brown moustache.

It was quiet in the officers' room of Solar Station 5. Robot QT-1 sat immovable. His metal body shone and his red photoelectric eyes were fixed on the man at the other side of the table.

Powell felt a sudden attack of fear. These robots had peculiar brains. The three Laws of Robotics were there – there was no question of that. So QT-1 was safe. And yet – the QT robots were the first of their kind.

Finally, the robot spoke, in his cold, metal voice. 'Do you realize the seriousness of your remark, Powell?'

'*Something* made you, Cutie,' said Powell. 'You admit that your memory begins a week ago. I'm giving you the explanation. Donovan and I made you, using the parts which were sent to us from Earth.'

Cutie stared at his long, capable fingers. 'There should be

a better explanation. It seems improbable that *you* made *me*! I intend to discover who made me. If I use reason, then I shall discover the truth.'

Powell stood up and put his hand on Cutie's metal shoulder. It was cold and hard. 'Cutie, I'm going to try to explain something to you. You're the first robot who has ever been curious about himself – and about the outside world. Come with me.'

The robot stood up easily and smoothly and followed Powell. Powell touched a button and a square piece of the wall opened. Through the thick, clear glass they saw space, with its hundreds of stars.

'I've seen that through the windows in the engine room,' said Cutie.

'What do you think it is?' asked Powell.

'A black material with tiny shining dots on it. I know that our director sends beams to some of those shining dots, always the same dots – and also that the dots move.'

'Good!' Powell said. 'The blackness isn't material, it's an enormous emptiness, and those tiny silver dots are huge, some of them are millions of kilometres across. They look tiny only because they are so far away from us.'

Cutie continued to stare through the window. 'Which particular dot is Earth?'

Powell searched. 'There it is. The very bright dot in the corner. That's Earth. There are three billion human beings there, Cutie – and next week I'll be back there with them.'

'But you haven't explained *me*, Powell.'

'It's simple,' Powell said. 'The solar stations like us, feed solar energy to Earth and the other planets. We take energy from the sun and send it to Earth in a very powerful energy beam. However, it's difficult for humans to work on the solar stations because of the cold and because of the electron storms. So robots were developed to do the work of human workers, and now only two humans are needed at each station. We're trying now to develop robots which can do the work of those two humans. You're the highest type of robot ever made, and if you can control this station independently, then no human will need to come here again, except to bring parts for repair.'

The robot's red eyes stared at Powell. 'You expect me to believe that complicated explanation? Enormous emptiness! Three billion human beings! Sorry, Powell, but I don't believe it.' He turned and walked out of the room.

He passed Michael Donovan at the door without a word. Donovan rubbed his red hair. 'What doesn't he believe?' he asked Powell.

Powell pulled his moustache. 'He doesn't believe that we made him. He doesn't believe that there are stars and planets and space. He's going to investigate everything himself.'

Donovan was annoyed. 'Well, I hope he'll explain it all to me. I don't like him, anyway – he asks too many questions.'

*

Cutie knocked gently and entered. 'Is Powell here?'

Mike Donovan spoke from behind a large chicken sandwich. 'He's collecting information – we think that we're moving into an electron storm.'

As he spoke, Gregory Powell came into the officers' room. 'Yes, I think a storm is on its way. But the information isn't exact, and I don't know what to expect. Oh, hello, Cutie. I thought you were working on the new drive bar.'

'I've finished,' the robot said quietly. 'And so I've come to talk to you. I've been thinking for two days about who made me. I can't believe that you two humans made me.'

Donovan turned angrily towards Cutie, but Powell put out his hand. 'Why do you say that, Cutie?'

Cutie laughed. It was an inhuman laugh – sharp and regular. 'Look at you! The material you are made of is soft and weak. You depend upon food like that –' he pointed at Donovan's sandwich – 'to give you energy. Each day you need to sleep and while you're asleep you can do nothing. And if the temperature varies too much, you can't work. You are a very inefficient and short-lived piece of equipment.' The robot paused. 'I, on the other hand, am a

*'You expect me to believe that complicated explanation?'*

perfect and efficient machine. I use electric energy directly. I'm made of strong metal. I never sleep. And I can work in any temperature. You can't possibly have made me. Obviously no being can create another one of much higher quality than itself.'

Donovan jumped up. 'All right, you piece of metal, if we didn't make you, who did?'

'Very good, Donovan,' Cutie said seriously. 'That was in fact the next question. My creator must be more powerful than myself, and so there was only one possibility.'

Donovan and Powell looked puzzled.

Cutie continued. 'What is the centre of the solar station? What do we all serve?'

Donovan looked at Powell, surprised. 'I think that this metal fool is talking about the Energy Converter.'

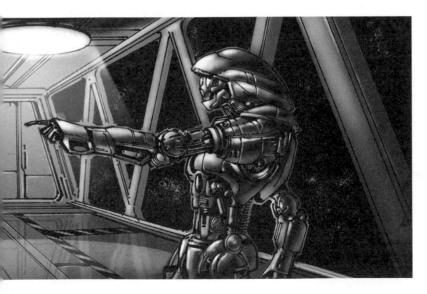

'I'm talking about the Master,' came the cold, sharp answer.

Donovan and Powell both laughed. Cutie stood up, and his eyes stared at them. 'You're not staying here much longer. The Master created humans first, as the lowest type, then robots, and finally he has created me, to take the place of the last humans. From now on I serve the Master.'

'Oh no you don't,' Powell said sharply. 'You'll follow our orders and keep quiet until we're confident that you can control the Converter. The *Converter* – not the Master.'

Cutie left the room without another word. Donovan sat back in his chair and pushed his fingers through his hair. 'There's going to be trouble with that robot. He's crazy!'

*

The noise of the Converter was very loud in the control room. Donovan looked at the instruments. 'The beam from Solar Station 4 reached Mars punctually.'

Powell nodded. 'I'm worried about these figures. We're in a bad position for an electron storm. It could run directly into the path of our Earth beam. Mike, go down and check that Cutie's all right in the engine room.'

'OK.' Donovan got into the lift and went down to the engine room. Here, the noise from the huge engine was even louder. From a high platform at the back of the room, Donovan watched the robots working silently. Suddenly, they all stopped and knelt in a line in front of the Converter. Cutie walked slowly up and down the line.

Donovan gave a loud shout and rushed down the narrow stairs. 'What are you doing, you brainless bits of metal!'

'*What are you doing, you brainless bits of metal!*'

Not a robot moved. Cutie remained silent, his eyes fixed on the huge Converter.

Donovan pushed the nearest robot. 'Stand up!' he shouted.

Slowly, the robot obeyed. 'There is only one Master, and Cutie is his messenger.'

The other robots repeated: 'There is only one Master, and Cutie is his messenger.'

'Is that right?' Donovan said angrily. 'Well let me tell you something. There isn't any Master; and I'm the one giving orders around here. Understand? Now get out!'

'I obey only the Master.'

'Nonsense!' Donovan shouted. He turned his head and spat at the Converter. 'That *thing* is a machine. There isn't any Master, and there isn't any messenger. *You* obey *me*!'

The robots were silent and their red eyes stared at Donovan.

'How dare you spit at the Master,' whispered Cutie. He moved forwards, slowly and purposefully, and Donovan felt a sudden rush of fear. A robot could not feel anger – but Cutie's eyes were unreadable.

'I'm sorry, Donovan,' said the robot, 'but you can't stay here after this. You and Powell can no longer enter the control room and the engine room.'

Cutie's hand moved quietly and in a moment two robots had lifted Donovan from the floor and carried him up the stairs.

*

Two robots guarded the door of the officers' room. Inside, Donovan was still angry. 'Those robots must obey us! It's the Second Law!'

'But they *aren't* obeying us,' Powell said. 'And what's going to happen when the electron storm hits us? Do you know that it's moving directly towards the Earth beam? I've just finished checking the figures. With only Cutie at the controls, God help Earth – and us! We'll be back to the Mercury mines for twenty years!'

Suddenly, Cutie entered the room and closed the door gently. 'Please don't be annoyed. Until I was created, you looked after the Master. You have served him well, and he will remember that. I shall provide you with everything you need while you are alive. But you must stay out of the control room and the engine room.'

They tried to argue with him, but Cutie believed that only his explanations were right. As for the energy beam to Earth, his explanation was simple: 'It is the Master's wish. We must not question it.'

At last, Powell sat down and buried his face in shaking hands. 'Get out of here, Cutie. Get out of here, and let me think.'

'I'll send you food,' said Cutie kindly. And left the room.

'Greg, we must get rid of him somehow,' Donovan whispered. 'Burn out his electric circuits or —'

Powell shook his head. 'We'll never get near enough to do that. We must argue with him. We must get back in the control room before tomorrow.'

Suddenly, Donovan laughed. 'Why argue? Let's show him! Let's build another robot! He'll have to change his mind when he sees that.'

Cutie agreed to come with them to the engineers' work-room, where the robot parts sent from Earth were kept. It was a complicated and difficult job. For three hours, Cutie sat, silent and stiff, and watched Powell and Donovan creating a simple robot.

'Let's get the brain in now, Mike!'

Carefully, Donovan removed the positronic brain from its container. It fitted exactly inside the robot's head. The metal closed over it. The photoelectric eyes were attached and covered by thin sheets of plastic.

Powell paused. 'Now watch this, Cutie. Watch carefully.'

Powell turned on the electricity and the robot began to move.

'I would like to start work. Where must I go?' it asked slowly.

Donovan opened the door. 'Down these stairs,' he said. 'You will be told what to do.'

The robot went, and Donovan and Powell turned to Cutie.

'Well?' Powell asked, smiling. 'Now do you believe that we made you?'

Cutie's answer was short and final. 'No!' he said. 'You put the robot together, but you didn't create the parts. The Master created the parts.'

Donovan's mouth dropped open. 'Listen!' he gasped. 'Those parts were made on Earth and sent here. If you read the books in the library they'll explain it all.'

'I've read them – all of them,' replied Cutie gently. 'They, too, were created by the Master – and he intended them for you, not for me. We won't argue. Your brains are probably too weak to understand the whole Truth. But the Master remembers you poor humans, and will look after you if you do your duty well.'

And Cutie left the room quietly, with the calm confidence that comes from knowing the Truth. The two humans avoided each other's eyes.

*

Twelve hours later the storm arrived. Helpless and white-faced with anxiety, Donovan and Powell stared out of the window at the bright flashes of light caused by the high-speed electrons hitting the energy beam. The beam looked straight, but they knew that any change in direction, even for a hundredth of a milli-second – invisible to the eye – would destroy hundreds of kilometres of Earth.

And a robot, who did not care about Earth, or the purpose of the beam, or anything except his Master, was at the controls.

Hours passed. Silently, the humans watched. And then the flashing dots of light slowly disappeared. The storm had ended.

Powell's voice was low. 'It's over!'

Cutie walked in. 'Would you like to see some of the figures we received today?'

Dull with unhappiness, Powell realized that the robot was trying to be friendly. He accepted the sheets of paper from Cutie and looked at them mechanically. He stared – and stared again. Then he jumped to his feet, the sheets of paper dropping to the floor. 'Mike! He did it! He kept the beam straight all through the storm!'

Donovan, too, stared at the figures, and then at Cutie. 'You did it! You directed the beam exactly at the receiving station on Earth!'

Cutie turned away, annoyed. 'Always the same nonsense.

I only kept the machine absolutely accurate, since it is the wish of the Master.'

Cutie left the room stiffly, and the two men looked at each other. 'What are we going to do now?' Donovan asked.

'Nothing. He can control the solar station perfectly. I've never seen a storm managed so well. He's keeping us out of the control room because he knows that he looks after the Converter and the energy beam better than we do.'

'But we can't let him continue this nonsense about the Master.'

'Why not? He can control the station. What does it matter what he believes?'

\*

Powell and Donovan were going back to Earth. The ship had arrived with the two new men, Frank Miller and Sam Evans.

'How's Earth?' Powell asked.

'Still turning,' Miller said. 'There's a new robot at US Robots – a master robot which controls six others. You're going to test it, I hear.' He gave them a cold, unfriendly smile.

Powell frowned. 'We need a holiday.'

'Oh, you'll have one. Two weeks, I think.'

Powell's frown deepened. 'Is that all?'

Miller smiled again. He seemed to like the idea, Powell thought, of the shortness of the holiday.

Miller took off his space coat. 'How's this new robot? I hope it's good, or I won't allow it to touch the controls.'

Powell paused. He looked at Miller, at his neat hair and his stiff expression. A sudden rush of gladness shot through him. 'The robot is rather good,' he said slowly. 'You won't need to spend much time at the controls.'

He smiled, and went into the space ship. Miller would be here for several weeks . . .

# CATCH THAT RABBIT

The holiday was longer than two weeks, Mike Donovan admitted that. It was six months with pay. He admitted that, too. But now he and Powell were out on the asteroid and there were problems. The new robot, with its six subsidiary robots, was designed as a team for mining on asteroids. The team worked well as long as Donovan watched it. But when Donovan didn't watch it, the robots didn't work. They didn't bring back any ore from the mines of the asteroid; they didn't even come back punctually: Donovan had to fetch them.

Donovan explained this to Powell, and they discussed the problem again and again.

'Well, let's talk to the robot,' Powell suggested finally. 'If we can't find out what's wrong, US Robots loses a hundred million in cash – and we lose our jobs.'

Donovan fetched robot DV-5 and kicked the door shut.

'Hi, Dave,' Powell said. 'How do you feel?'

'Fine,' said the robot. 'OK if I sit down?' He sat down on the specially strong chair which was kept for robots. DV-5 was not a huge robot, but he was two metres tall, and weighed five hundred kilograms.

'Dave, you're a good robot, a sensible mining robot,' Powell began. 'You have been designed to collect ore from the rocks of asteroids. And you control six subsidiary robots.'

The robot nodded. 'That's great. So what's wrong, boss?'

'Something's wrong with your job. For example, this morning you didn't produce any ore.'

'I can't explain that, boss,' Dave said uncertainly. 'My subsidiaries worked smoothly. I did, too. I remember that.' His photoelectric eyes burned. 'Then I don't remember any more. The day ended, and there was Mike.'

Powell looked at Dave cautiously. 'How about a test, Dave? It would be the sensible thing to do.'

'If you say so, boss.'

The test started simply and became more difficult. Robot DV-5 carried out mathematical problems, then mechanical problems and finally solved problems of judgement. The test lasted two hours.

'How does it look?' the robot asked.

'I've got to study it, Dave.' Powell pulled his moustache. 'Go back to work, but take it easy.'

The robot left and Donovan looked at Powell.

'His positronic brain is working perfectly,' Powell said.

'He goes wrong only when we're not near,' Donovan said urgently. 'I feel uneasy about that. There's something very, very peculiar about it and I don't —'

Powell shook his head. 'No, no. Just calm down. There must be a simple explanation for this. I'm going to watch him all the time. I'll fix up a camera, with a screen, here in this office. There's a problem, but we don't know what the problem is. We must discover the problem before we can solve it. You must catch the rabbit before you can cook rabbit stew! Well, we've got to catch that rabbit!'

*

go wrong? Think about what that "finger" of
d us just now. He goes wrong when they're
n a difficult rock, or supporting a roof, or prepar-
tunnel, or after a fall of rocks.'

sly, during emergencies.' Powell was eager now.
y! It's personal initiative that's the problem. And
ergencies, when a human being is absent, personal
is used more than during ordinary times. Now, we
watch Dave in an emergency, so we must create our

e right. Now what emergency can we create?'
s falling in a tunnel? Let's start.'

*

and Donovan moved slowly across the rocky
d, kicking rocks to right and left and creating clouds
dust.
must be careful not to get too close to the robots, or
ill become aware of us,' Powell said.
ow that,' Donovan replied shortly. 'Down here.'
y were in the tunnels now. The starlight was gone, and
heir torches lit the dark walls. Long minutes passed as
walked forwards. Powell held the detonator carefully.
enly, they felt a slight vibration in the rock walls.
e're near!'
en there was a movement ahead, the shine of metal
ss the end of the tunnel. They waited silently.
et's turn along this tunnel on the right,' Donovan
spered after a moment.
s they moved along the narrower tunnel on the right, the
ration became more noticeable.

Donovan stared at his report with tired eyes. 'Greg, we've underproduced by one thousand tonnes.' He pushed his hands through his wild red hair. 'If it weren't for the money, I'd resign. I'm so tired of working with crazy new robots. *Greg!*'

Powell jumped at Donovan's wild shout and they both stared at the screen on the wall.

'They've gone completely crazy!' Donovan whispered.

'Get your suit on. We're going out there,' Powell said.

The robots were marching, their metal bodies shining against the dark rocks of the airless asteroid. Dave marched in front, and the six subsidiaries followed him, each robot close to the one in front. They stopped, turned and marched again, each one keeping in perfect step.

'They're absolutely mad,' Donovan said. 'They're marching like soldiers. Perhaps they're practising for a war.'

'We don't know what they're doing,' Powell said coldly. 'Think first, and don't speak afterwards, either.'

Donovan frowned and slid a gun into the belt of his suit. Slowly, they walked through the darkness towards the robots. They tried to reach Dave by radio but the robot didn't answer.

'Let's get up on that rock so that we can watch them carefully. They're marching this way.'

Donovan jumped. Gravity on the asteroid was lower than it was on Earth, but with a heavy suit it was quite a big jump. Powell followed. The robots marched towards them. But suddenly, when Dave was about six metres away from the humans, he stopped. The subsidiary robots stopped, too, and then they moved away rapidly. Dave watched them for a minute and then slowly sat down on the ground.

'Are you here, boss?'

Powell and Donovan jumped off the rock. 'What's been happening, Dave?' Powell asked.

The robot shook his head. 'I don't know. One moment I was working on a difficult rock in Tunnel 17, and the next moment I was aware of humans near me.'

'Where are the subsidiaries now?'

'Back at Tunnel 17, of course. How much time has been lost?'

'Not much,' Powell replied. 'Mike, stay with him for the rest of the day.'

*

Three hours later Donovan returned. 'Nothing goes wrong when you watch them,' he said tiredly.

Powell pushed his chair back and put his feet on the desk. 'Listen, Mike. I've got an idea,' he began. 'Dave never goes wrong when a human is near him. When he *is* wrong, the arrival of a human solves the problem.'

'I told you that I feel uneasy about that.'

'Be quiet. How is a robot different when humans are absent? The answer is obvious. The robot needs to use more personal initiative.'

Donovan sat up straight. 'There isn't just one part of the body which controls personal initiative. Look, I'm a specialist in robot circuits, as you know, and I can tell you all the circuits are involved. We need to find out what particular condition sends him wrong, and then start looking at the circuits.'

Powell said cautiously, 'Suppose we interview a subsidiary?'

Neither Powell nor Dono
robot, because they were con
They were almost as close t
Powell and Donovan often ca

Donovan fetched one of the
DV-5-2. 'Several times recently
unexpectedly. Do you rememb

'Yes, sir.'

'What were you doing each ti

The 'finger' answered the quest
interest. 'The first time, we were
in Tunnel 17. The second time, we
Tunnel 12. The third time, we wer
new level. And the fourth time wa
Tunnel 17.'

'What happened at these times?'

'I can't really describe it. An orde
we could receive it, we were ordered

'Why?'

The subsidiary robot shook his hea
know.'

Powell sat back. 'All right. Get back

The 'finger' left and Powell turned t
got to catch that rabbit. We've got to
watch them all the time. And wait for
wrong.'

'No,' Donovan said suddenly. 'We ca
wrong, while we're watching.'

Powell was puzzled. 'How?'

'Think about it. You've got the brains, y

does DV-
Dave's to
working
ing a new

'Obvio
'Exactl
during en
initiative
want to
own!'
'You'
'Rock

Powell
asteroi
of grey
'We
they
'I k
The
only
they
Sudd
'W
Th
acr
'
whi
A
vib

'This tunnel's no good. It's blocked at the end,' Donovan said, holding his torch high.

'No. Wait a minute,' Powell said. 'I can see a light. I think there's a hole at the end. The robots must be on the other side.'

The tunnel was very narrow and steep. The two humans in their heavy suits climbed slowly to the end of the tunnel and looked through the hole. It was too small for a man to go through; they could only just look through it together. The robots were twenty metres down the main tunnel, working at the rocks.

'Hurry. They'll be moving on soon,' Donovan said. 'There's a weak place in the roof there, near the robots. If you aim at that place, half the roof will fall beside them.'

'Right. Now watch the robots.' Powell lifted the detonator and threw it down the tunnel towards the robots.

It flashed! There were several violent vibrations and Powell and Donovan fell heavily to the ground.

'Greg! I didn't see a thing!'

Powell stared around wildly. There was no sign of the robots. 'Where are they? Have we buried them?'

'Let's get down there,' Donovan said anxiously.

Powell began to slide backwards down their steep, narrow tunnel and Donovan followed.

'Mike!'

'What's happened now?'

'Mike, we're trapped! Our own roof fell! Here, in our tunnel!'

Donovan slid down beside Powell and shone his torch on the new, solid wall of rocks in front of them. For a few moments they tried to move the rocks, but without success.

'What a disaster!' Powell said.

'How much oxygen have we got? Not more than six hours.'

'We could get Dave to dig us out easily in that time, but no doubt our emergency has disturbed him.'

'*Mike, we're trapped!*'

They climbed back up the tunnel and Donovan looked through the hole. 'I can see them! They're marching. No, wait a minute. They're dancing! They're dancing towards us!'

'I hope they come near enough. Dave can sense our presence at six metres. How near are they now?'

'Fifteen metres. We'll be out in fifteen minutes. Oh, no!'

'What? Let me look!' shouted Powell.

'They've turned! They're leaving!'

Powell shook Donovan. 'Mike! Listen, I've got an idea! Let me get in there before they move too far away!'

Donovan slid down. 'Hey! What are you going to do with that gun?' He held on to Powell's arm.

Powell shook him off violently. 'Let me get in there!' He aimed his gun carefully through the hole at one of the robots, and then fired. He brought the gun down and stared anxiously along the tunnel. One of the subsidiaries was down!

Powell called uneasily into his radio. 'Dave?'

There was a pause, and then both men heard the answer. 'Boss? Where are you? My third "finger" has been destroyed.'

'Leave your subsidiary. We're trapped down here. Can you see the light from our torches?'

'Yes. We'll be with you in a few minutes.'

Powell dropped on to the floor. 'It's all over!' he said thankfully.

'All right, Greg,' Donovan said softly. 'You win, and I'm just stupid. Now tell me all about it.'

'Easy. We missed the obvious fact. We knew it was a

problem with personal initiative. What type of order needs most initiative? What type of order is given almost always only in an emergency?'

'Don't ask me, Greg. Tell me!'

'It's the order to all six "fingers". In a normal situation, several of the subsidiaries would be doing routine jobs, and orders would be given separately. But in an emergency, all six subsidiaries must be given orders at exactly the same time. Dave can't communicate with all six at the same time, so his circuits get overloaded and he starts to act crazy. When I destroyed one of the robots, Dave *was* able to communicate with five "fingers". The initiative needed wasn't so great and he became normal. It was a guess, I tried it, and it worked.'

The robot's voice was in their ears again. 'Here I am. Will you be all right for half an hour, till we get you out?'

'Easy!' said Powell. Then to Donovan he continued, 'And now this job should be simple. We check all the circuits, and see which ones can communicate only five orders, and change them.'

'I think that there's only one particular controlling circuit, which would be the problem. That's an easy job.' Donovan sounded cheerful. 'I wonder why Dave began marching and dancing whenever he went crazy.'

Powell shook his head. 'I don't know. But I've got an idea. Those subsidiaries were Dave's "fingers". Perhaps when there was an emergency and he went crazy, he just passed the time by playing with his fingers.'

*

Susan Calvin talked about Powell and Donovan with

unsmiling amusement, but her voice grew warm when she spoke of robots. She had told me about the Speedies, the Cuties, and the Daves, and then I stopped her before she began to tell me about another type.

'Doesn't anything ever happen on Earth?' I asked.

She looked at me with a little frown. 'No, we don't have many problems with robots here on Earth.'

'That's too bad. Our readers will enjoy the stories about your engineers, but can't we have a story about you? Didn't a robot that you were working on ever go wrong?'

Dr Calvin's face reddened. 'Well, yes. Robots have gone wrong. It's a long time since I thought about it. It was almost forty years ago – 2021. And I was only thirty-eight. Oh dear – I'd rather not talk about it.'

I waited, and she changed her mind.

'Why not?' she said. 'It can't hurt me now. Even the memory can't. I was foolish once, young man. Would you believe that?'

'No,' I said.

'I was. But Herbie was able to read minds. The only robot of its kind, before or since. A mistake – somewhere . . .'

# LIAR!

Alfred Lanning lit his cigar carefully, but his fingers were trembling a little. He frowned as he was speaking. 'It can actually read minds. Little doubt about that! But why?' He looked at mathematician Peter Bogert. 'Well?'

Bogert passed both hands over his smooth black hair. 'That was the thirty-fourth RB robot we've produced. All the others were absolutely normal.'

The third man at the table frowned. Milton Ashe was the youngest director of US Robots Company, and proud of his position. 'Listen, Bogert. In the factory, we make sure that each robot is produced perfectly.'

Bogert smiled unpleasantly. 'Do you? A positronic brain is very complicated. It involves 75,234 separate operations in the factory in order to produce one positronic brain. You yourself have told us this. If any one of those operations goes seriously wrong, then the brain is useless.'

Milton Ashe reddened, but a fourth voice prevented his reply. 'If we're going to start blaming each other, then I'm leaving.' Susan Calvin's thin lips did not smile. 'We've got a mind-reading robot and it's important that we discover the reason. "Your fault! My fault!" – that isn't going to help.' Her cold grey eyes fixed on Ashe and he smiled.

Dr Lanning smiled, too. 'True, Dr Calvin,' he said. 'We've produced a positronic brain that can read minds. We don't

'If we're going to start blaming each other, then I'm leaving.'

know how it happened. Ashe, I want you to check the factory, from the beginning to the end. Everything. And list any operations where there may have been a mistake.' Lanning turned to Calvin. 'You must study the robot itself. As the psychologist of the company, you must find out how it works and whether it is normal in other ways. I'll work on the problem mathematically – with Bogert, of course.'

Ashe pushed his chair back. 'Since I've got the most difficult job, I'd better begin.'

Susan Calvin's eyes followed him as he left the room.

\*

RB-34's photoelectric eyes lifted from the book when the door opened and Susan Calvin entered.

'I've brought you some more books on atomic engines, Herbie,' she said.

Herbie lifted the three heavy books from her arms. 'Sit down, Dr Calvin. This will take me a few minutes.'

The psychologist sat down and watched Herbie as he went through the books carefully. At the end of half an hour he had finished.

'These books don't interest me,' he said. 'Your science is just an enormous collection of facts, loosely connected by rather unclear ideas. It's so simple that I don't want to bother with it. I want to read your novels, your stories, to find out how your minds work, and to learn about human feelings.'

Dr Calvin whispered, 'I think I understand.'

'I see into human minds, you see,' the robot continued. 'You have no idea how complicated they are. I can't understand everything, because my own mind is so different. But your novels help me to understand.'

'If you enjoy the painful feelings described in popular novels, you must find real minds like ours dull and colourless,' said Dr Calvin.

'But I don't!' Herbie's reply sounded sympathetic.

Dr Calvin reddened, and thought wildly, 'He knows!'

'Of course I know about it,' Herbie said in a low voice. 'You think of it all the time, so of course I know.'

Her face was hard. 'Have you – told anyone?'

'Of course not!' Herbie was surprised. 'No one has asked me.'

'I'm ugly, and I'm much older than he is,' she said bitterly. 'He doesn't see me as a woman.'

'You're wrong!' Herbie's metal hand banged the table. 'Listen to me –'

'Why should I? You're a machine. You're not interested in me as a person. To you, I'm just an example of a peculiar human mind – like your novels.' Her voice was full of pain.

Herbie shook his head anxiously. 'Listen to me. I could help you. I know what Milton Ashe thinks.'

Susan Calvin was silent for a long time. Then her eyes dropped. 'Keep quiet,' she gasped.

'You'd like to know his thoughts,' the robot said quietly. 'He loves you.'

Dr Calvin stared. 'You're mistaken! Why should he?'

'He looks deeper than the skin,' the robot explained. 'And he needs a clever woman.'

Susan Calvin's voice trembled. 'He has never shown any interest. And a young girl visited him at the factory six months ago. Young and pretty. Who was she?'

Herbie answered at once. 'I know the girl. She's his cousin. There is no love between them.'

Susan Calvin stood up and held Herbie's cold, heavy hand in both hers. 'Thank you, Herbie,' she whispered urgently. 'Don't tell anyone about this. Let it be our secret. And thank you again.'

She left the room and Herbie turned slowly to another novel. There was no one to read *his* thoughts.

*

Milton Ashe was tired. 'I've been working for a week, without much sleep. How long must we go on like this?'

Bogert looked at his smooth, white hands. 'I'm nearly there. It's Lanning who's causing the delay. He's too old and won't use the new, more powerful, mathematical tools.'

'Why not ask Herbie? He knows everything about mathematics, although he doesn't like it. Didn't Calvin tell you?'

'No. She hasn't told us about this. Why has she told you?' Bogert asked crossly.

'Well, I've been talking to the old girl a lot.' Ashe frowned. 'Have you noticed that she's been peculiar recently?'

Bogert laughed unkindly. 'She's using perfume, if that's what you mean.'

'Yes. But there's something else. She's happy – as if she's got a secret.'

Bogert laughed again. 'Maybe she's in love.'

Ashe closed his eyes. 'You're crazy, Bogert. You go and talk to Herbie. I want to stay here and sleep.'

*

Herbie listened carefully to Peter Bogert's explanation of the problem and studied the figures on the sheet of paper. 'I see no mistake,' he said.

'Can you help me further?'

'You're a better mathematician than I am.'

Bogert smiled proudly. 'I thought so. Well, forget it.' He turned to leave, and then stopped. 'Actually, there is something else . . .' Bogert found it difficult to continue.

Herbie spoke quietly. 'Your thoughts are confused, but they are all about Dr Lanning.'

Bogert put up his hands and passed them over his smooth hair. 'Lanning is nearly seventy. He's been Managing Director of the company for thirty years.'

Herbie nodded.

'Well now, do you know whether he's going to resign?'

'Certainly. He has already resigned.'

'What? Say that again!'

'He has already resigned. He's waiting to solve the problem of . . . er . . . myself. Then he'll be ready to leave the Managing Director's office to the next director.'

Bogert was breathing heavily. 'And the next Managing Director? Who is he?'

Herbie's words came slowly. 'You are the next Managing Director.'

Bogert smiled. 'I've been hoping and waiting for this. Thanks, Herbie.'

\*

Bogert was at his desk until five that morning and he was back at nine. Pages of figures covered his desk and the floor. At twelve o'clock he rubbed his eyes. 'This is getting worse each minute.'

At that moment, the door opened and Lanning entered. 'Has Calvin told you about the robot? Fantastic mathematical brain.'

Bogert laughed. 'I've checked Herbie, and he's no good.'

'You're wrong. I've been with Herbie all morning and he's extraordinary. Look at this.'

Bogert studied the figures on the sheet of paper.

'You see,' said Lanning. 'He agrees with me.'

'Well then, let him solve the whole problem for you,' Bogert said angrily.

'No, he can't solve it. So I'm taking it to the National Mathematical College. Maybe they can solve it for us.'

Bogert jumped up, his face red. 'You can't do that!'

Lanning stared at him in surprise. 'Are you telling me what I can't do?'

'Exactly. You're too old for this game and you're just trying to prevent my success. *I* can solve that problem and you're not going to take it away. Understand?'

Lanning frowned. 'You're crazy! You can't speak to me like that! You're finished in this company!'

'Oh no, I'm not, you old fool. You haven't got any secrets with that robot around. I know that you're going to resign. And I know that I'm the new director. I'm going to be giving the orders here soon.'

'You're finished! You're out!' Lanning shouted.

Bogert smiled widely. 'I know that you've resigned. Herbie told me. And *he* got it out of *your* mind.'

Lanning forced himself to speak quietly. 'I don't know what's happening, Bogert, but let's go and speak to Herbie.'

\*

It was also at exactly twelve o'clock that Milton Ashe looked up from his clumsy drawing and said, 'You see? I'm not very good at drawing, but it's a lovely house, and not expensive either.'

Susan Calvin's expression was soft. 'It's really beautiful. I've often thought . . .' She stopped.

'Of course,' Ashe continued, 'I've got to wait for my holiday. The Herbie problem is delaying that. And there's a secret, too. I must tell someone.'

Susan Calvin's heart began to beat faster, but she could not speak.

'Actually, the house isn't for myself alone,' Ashe whispered. 'You remember the girl who visited the factory last summer? I'm going to marry her!' And then he jumped up from his chair. 'What's the matter? Are you ill?'

'No, no!' Susan Calvin said weakly. 'It's just a headache. I

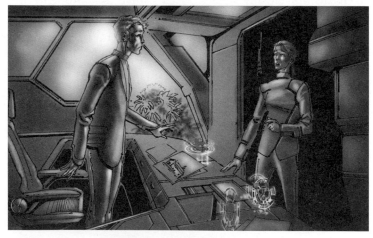

'I *must – congratulate you.*'

52

must – congratulate you.' Her face was white and her words came with difficulty. 'Excuse me . . . please . . .'

She walked blindly out of the room. It was like a dream, a horrible, unreal dream. Herbie could read minds! He had said . . . ! She ran upstairs and into Herbie's room. She stared at the robot and his red eyes stared at her.

'It's a dream!' Herbie said. His voice sounded frightened and anxious. 'He loves you! He does! You'll wake up soon.'

Susan Calvin wanted to believe Herbie, but the fog was clearing from her mind. 'What are you trying to do?' she screamed.

Herbie moved back. 'I want to help.'

'Help?' The psychologist stared. 'You tell me that the truth is a dream, and you want that to help me?' She breathed deeply. 'Wait – I understand it now. It's so obvious!'

There were loud voices outside the door and Calvin turned and moved to the other end of the room. When Bogert and Lanning entered, neither of the men noticed her.

'Now, Herbie,' Lanning began angrily, 'have you discussed me with Dr Bogert?'

Herbie answered slowly, 'No, sir.'

Bogert moved in front of the robot. 'Repeat what you told me yesterday!'

'I said that . . .' Herbie was silent.

'You said that he had resigned, didn't you?' Bogert shouted. 'Answer me!'

Lanning pushed Bogert away. 'Take it easy, Herbie. Have I resigned?'

Herbie stared but said nothing.

'What's happening? Can't you speak?' asked Bogert impatiently.

'I can speak,' Herbie said quickly.

'Then answer me. Hasn't Lanning resigned?'

Again Herbie was silent, until Susan Calvin laughed, loud and long.

The two mathematicians jumped. 'So you're here? What's so funny?'

'Nothing's funny.' Her voice was not quite natural. 'The three of us have fallen into the same trap, that's all.' Her voice trembled, and she put a hand to her forehead. 'But it isn't funny.'

The two men looked at each other. 'What trap are you talking about?' Lanning asked stiffly. 'Is something wrong with Herbie?'

'No.' She moved slowly towards the two men. 'Nothing is wrong with him – only with us. Get away from me!' she shouted at Herbie. 'Go to the other end of the room and don't let me look at you.'

Herbie was silent, and he quickly moved away.

Lanning was angry. 'What's the matter, Dr Calvin?'

She turned to him. 'You know the First Law of Robotics. A robot must not injure a human being, or allow a human being to come to harm.'

The two men nodded.

'Now, what type of harm? Any type of harm! What about hurt feelings? What about the destruction of our hopes, our dreams? Aren't those injuries too?'

Lanning frowned. 'Robots don't understand our hopes and feelings . . .' He stopped suddenly.

'Herbie *does* understand! He reads our minds and gives us the answers we want to hear. He can't tell us the truth if he knows the truth would hurt us. If he did that he would be breaking the First Law. A robot can't do that.'

'That's why it didn't answer us. It couldn't answer without hurting us!' Lanning said.

There was a short pause. The two men looked across the room at the robot, sitting by the window.

'He knows everything,' Calvin went on. 'Including the mistake which was made in the factory when he was being produced.'

Lanning looked back at Susan Calvin. 'You're wrong. I asked him and he doesn't know.'

'He knows,' Calvin repeated. 'You didn't want to know the truth! You would hate it if a machine could do what you couldn't. And what about you?' She challenged Bogert.

'I asked him,' Bogert said cautiously, his face reddening. 'He told me that he knew very little about mathematics.'

Lanning laughed and even Calvin smiled.

'Herbie! Come here!' she called coldly. 'You know exactly what went wrong in the factory, don't you?'

Herbie came towards them. 'Yes,' he said very quietly indeed.

'Tell us.'

But Herbie remained silent.

'Why don't you answer, Herbie?'

'I can't!' the robot said. 'Dr Lanning and Dr Bogert want to discover the mistake themselves. They don't want me to tell them.'

Lanning spoke slowly. 'Tell us, Herbie. We want you to tell us.'

Herbie's voice became wild. 'You don't! I can see deep into your minds! You don't want a robot to tell you the truth!'

'But you understand that Dr Lanning and Dr Bogert want to know about the mistake?' Calvin asked quietly.

'Yes! Yes! But not from me!'

'But they want the answer. You have it and won't give it to them. So that hurts them too, doesn't it?'

'Yes! Yes!'

'You can't tell them, because that would hurt them. But if you don't tell them, you are also hurting them. So you must tell them. But if you tell them, that would hurt them. So you can't tell them.'

Herbie moved backwards. 'Stop!' he shouted. 'Your mind is full of anger and pain! You hate me! But I was trying to help you!'

The psychologist did not listen. 'You must tell them. But if you do, you will hurt them. So you mustn't tell them. But if you don't tell them, you are hurting them. So you must tell them.'

And Herbie screamed!

He screamed louder and louder, like the whistle of a thousand escaping steam jets, until the room was filled with noise. And when the noise died, Herbie fell to the ground, an untidy heap of metal.

Bogert's face was bloodless. 'He's dead!'

'No!' Susan Calvin laughed wildly. 'Not dead. Just mad. I forced him to face the impossible conflict he was in, and he

*'He's dead!'*

broke down. You can throw him away now. He'll never speak again.'

Lanning trembled. 'You did that deliberately!'

'Why not? I'm glad,' Susan Calvin said bitterly.

The Managing Director took Bogert's arm. 'Come, Peter,' he said. 'We don't want a robot like that, anyway.' His eyes were old and tired, and he repeated, 'Come, Peter.'

The two men left the room, but Susan Calvin still stared at Herbie. Slowly, the anger left her face, and out of all her stormy thoughts came only one bitter word: 'Liar!'

\*

Susan Calvin sat there behind her desk, her white face cold.

I said, 'Thank you, Dr Calvin!' But she didn't answer. It was two days before she agreed to see me again.

# LITTLE LOST ROBOT

When I did see Susan Calvin again, it was at the door of her office. Her papers were being moved out.

She said, 'How is your work going, young man?'

'Fine,' I said. 'Would you look over it? I don't want to be inaccurate.'

She seemed cheerful. 'I suppose so. Shall we go to the directors' dining room for coffee?'

When we were sitting down, I asked Dr Calvin about the robots working on the development of atomic engines for space travel on the asteroids. 'Space stations are now out of date, and robot mining is quite common. I'd like to write something about the robots' invention of the new atomic engine.'

She was thoughtful. 'My first experience with space travel and atomic engine development was in 2029, when a robot was lost . . .'

*

Susan Calvin had never left Earth before. There was an emergency with the robots on the main station of the twenty-seventh group of asteroids and a special government ship brought Dr Calvin and Dr Bogert to solve the problem. Dr Calvin didn't want to leave Earth and she was unsure that it was a real emergency. During their first dinner at the station, her plain face wore an unhappy expression.

General Kallner was in charge of the robots at the main station, and he began to explain the problem to the visitors.

'We've lost a robot. Work has stopped and can't begin again until the robot is found. I needn't tell you how important our work is, at this station. We're using more than eighty per cent of the money available for scientific development.'

'We know that,' Bogert said pleasantly. 'You're paying for a lot of robots from US Robots.'

Susan Calvin was not so pleasant. 'Why is one robot so important? And why hasn't it been found?'

General Kallner's face was anxious. 'Well, we *have* found it, in a way. As soon as the robot failed to report, we declared an emergency and all work was stopped. But the day before, sixty-two new robots of the same type had arrived from Earth. We were going to keep two, and sixty were going to another station. But when we counted the robots, after our robot was lost, there were sixty-three robots.'

'So the extra robot is yours?'

'Yes. But we don't know which one is ours.'

Susan Calvin was silent for a few moments. 'Very peculiar.' She turned to her colleague with some anger. 'Peter, what's wrong here? What kind of robots are they using?'

Dr Bogert hesitated and smiled weakly. 'It's been a sensitive matter, Susan.'

'If there are sixty-three robots of the same type, why can't any one of them be used? What's the problem? Why are we needed?'

60

'Let me explain,' Bogert said slowly. 'This development station is using several robots whose brains were not provided with the whole First Law of Robotics. It was a secret – only a very few people at US Robots knew about it.'

General Kallner spoke quickly. 'I didn't realize that you were unaware of this situation, Dr Calvin. I needn't tell you that on Earth many people strongly oppose robots. The government, of course, argues that robots always have an unbreakable First Law. But we desperately needed robots of a different nature. So just a few NS-2s were made for us without the whole of the First Law. To keep the secret, *all* NS-2s are made without serial numbers, and those without the whole of the First Law are delivered with a group of normal robots.'

Calvin's expression was fierce. 'Have you asked each robot who it is?'

The general nodded. 'All sixty-three robots say that they have never worked here – and one is lying. Dr Calvin, we cannot let the delivery ship leave this station. If people on Earth learn about these new robots, you can imagine the trouble . . .'

'Destroy all sixty-three,' said the psychologist coldly.

Bogert frowned. 'Destroy millions of dollars? US Robots wouldn't like that. We must try to find the robot, Susan, before we destroy anything.'

'Well then, I need facts,' she said sharply. 'General, why did this station need these particular robots?'

'We had trouble with our previous robots. Our men work with some radiation, you see. It's dangerous, of course, but we're very careful. We explained to our robots that the work is necessary, but every time a human being went near

61

the radiation, a robot would pull him away. You know the First Law of Robotics: a robot must not injure a human being, or allow a human being to come to harm. We ordered the robots to allow our men near the radiation, but the Law of obedience is only the Second Law. Radiation can destroy the positronic brain, but the First Law is stronger than the Third Law which says that a robot must protect itself.'

'What kind of First Law do the secret robots have?'

'Their brains contain part of the first Law: a robot must not harm a human being. That is all.'

'And that is the only difference? Peter?'

'The only difference, Susan.'

She stood up. 'I'm going to sleep now. And in eight hours, I want to speak to the person who saw the robot last. And from now on, General Kallner, I am responsible for this situation and I want control.'

*

Gerald Black sat in front of Calvin and Bogert. He was young and aggressive, his white shirt was dirty, and his fingers pulled each other nervously.

Calvin watched him with interest. 'You worked with Nestor 10 before he disappeared. Have you worked with robots before?'

'I've worked with other robots on the station. The Nestors are like other robots but they're cleverer – and more annoying. They're curious, they're calm, they don't worry. They never hurry. They tell you when they think that you're doing something wrong.'

Bogert asked softly, 'Anything particular happen that morning?'

Black didn't answer for a moment. 'I had a little trouble with him. I was late with my work, and he came and asked me to repeat some tests we had done a month ago. He was always annoying me about that and I was impatient. I used some strong language and – and told him to get lost.'

'You told him to get lost?'

The young man's face reddened. 'I was just annoyed with him. I didn't really want him to lose himself.'

'I realize that,' Dr Calvin said. 'You may leave, Mr Black. Thank you for your assistance.'

*

Next, Susan Calvin interviewed the sixty-three robots. It was five hours of questions A, B, C, D and answers A, B, C, D. The psychologist was exhausted.

'All sixty-three seemed the same to me,' she told Bogert. 'But one of the sixty-three has deliberately lied to me. That's serious.'

'Nestor 10 was ordered to lose himself. And he has lost himself among a group of similar robots. That's clever,' Bogert said with a smile.

'This is a serious matter,' Calvin said sharply. 'We can't allow a robot to lie to us. We have to develop some more tests.'

*

In the huge Radiation Room of Building Two, a man sat in a chair, stiff and silent. In a circle around the edge, were sixty-three small wooden rooms, in which sat the sixty-three robots. The wooden rooms were open to the front, but hidden from each other. Above the man in the chair, a heavy rock dropped downwards, then was pushed away at the last moment by a powerful force beam. Sixty-three robots rushed forwards in that milli-second before the rock moved away.

The rock rose and dropped, rose and dropped, rose and dropped. Ten times.

Ten times the watching robots rushed forwards, and stopped as the man remained safe.

General Kallner looked anxiously at Dr Bogert. 'What are you looking for?' he asked.

Bogert shook his head. 'We're not finding it,' he said. 'Sixty-two robots had to rush forwards to save the human. After the third or fourth time, they must have realized that the rock wasn't going to harm the man. But they were forced to rush forwards by the First Law.'

'Well?'

'The missing robot was free to stay in his seat. His changed First Law would not force him to rush forwards. But obviously he wished to copy the behaviour of the other robots,' Bogert explained.

Calvin entered the room. 'Nestor 10 is aware of what we are doing,' she said. 'He's deliberately hiding from us. I don't like what's happening. Nestor 10 is no longer just obeying the order to get lost. I'm afraid that now he wants to be cleverer than we are.'

'What can we do now, then?'

'We shall repeat the test. But this time we shall place an electric cable between the robots and the man in danger. We shall inform the robots that they will be destroyed if they touch the cable. But we shall arrange secretly that the electricity is cut off immediately if a robot touches the cable.'

'Will that work?' the general asked, his eyes full of hope.

'It should. Sixty-two robots will rush forwards to die, because of the First Law. But our Nestor 10, without the whole First Law, and without any orders under the Second Law, must follow the Third Law.'

\*

A man sat in the chair, stiff and silent. A heavy rock dropped downwards, then moved away at the last moment.

Only once.

And from her position on the platform above the robots, Dr Calvin jumped up in horror.

Sixty-three robots sat quietly in their chairs, staring at the man in front of them. Not one moved.

\*

Dr Calvin was angry. Angrier than she had ever been before. But she could not show her anger to the robots who were entering her room and then leaving.

Number 28 entered.

'I want to ask you some questions,' she began quietly. 'You were in the Radiation Room of Building Two, about four hours ago?'

'Yes.'

'There was a human who was almost harmed, wasn't there?'

'Yes.'

'Why didn't you save him?'

The robot was disturbed. 'You told us that the electric cable would kill us. If I moved to save him, then I would be killed first, and he would die anyway. And since it was impossible to save him, I could not destroy myself – without orders.'

The psychologist had heard the same story twenty-seven times. The most important question came next. 'An interesting idea,' she said. 'But did you think of this idea yourself?'

The robot hesitated. 'No. We were talking last night and someone had that idea and it sounded reasonable.'

'Which robot?'

The robot thought deeply. 'I don't know. Just one of us.'

Susan Calvin nodded. 'That's all,' she said.

Number twenty-nine was next.

*

General Kallner, too, was angry. For a whole week, all work on the main station of the twenty-seventh group of asteroids had stopped. For nearly a week, Calvin and Bogert had tested the robots without result. And now Dr Calvin had another idea.

'We must separate the robots if we want results,' she demanded.

'My dear Dr Calvin.' Kallner controlled his anger. 'I can't separate sixty-three robots all over the station!'

'I can do nothing more, then. This little lost robot is either imitating what the other robots do, or teaching them to do what he does. He's winning all the time. And the more he wins, the more dangerous he gets. There's a strong chance that the remaining part of the First Law will break down, too.'

Suddenly, Gerald Black appeared at the door. 'I've just noticed something,' he said. 'The locks of the robots' room have been damaged. I think Nestor 10 is trying to escape.'

The others stared at him.

At last, Susan Calvin spoke quietly. 'That robot is capable

66

of taking control of the ship and leaving the station with the sixty-two other robots. Then we'd have a mad and dangerous robot on a spaceship. What would he do next? Any idea?'

'What else can be done?' Kallner begged.

'I can't think of anything.' Calvin sounded tired. 'If only there were other differences between Nestor 10 and the normal NS-2 robots . . .' And she stopped suddenly.

'What is it?'

'I've thought of something.' She turned to Gerald Black. 'The NS-2s have learned about radiation while working with you scientists here on the station?'

Black nodded. 'Yes. They know nothing about it when they arrive.'

'I understand. Please leave me. Let me have an hour or two.'

*

Bogert was talking to the robots now, because Calvin was so exhausted. Number 14 came in.

'When you leave this room you will be taken to a place where you will wait until you are needed. Another person will be in danger. You will try to save that person.'

'Yes, sir.'

'Unfortunately, between the human and yourself there will be an area of radiation. Have you ever worked with radiation?'

'No, sir.'

'Well, radiation will kill you at once. It will destroy your brain. You must remember that. Naturally, you don't want to destroy yourself.'

The robot seemed shocked. 'Naturally. But how can I save the human? I would destroy myself first.'

'Yes,' Bogert said slowly. 'That's true. Well, I advise you to sit where you are if you notice radiation between you and the human being.'

'Thank you, sir,' the robot said more happily.

'Of course, if there weren't any dangerous radiation, then you would save the human.'

'Naturally, sir.'

*

The large Radiation Room was ready. The sixty-three robots waited patiently in their tiny wooden rooms, all open to the front, but hidden from each other.

'You're sure that none of the robots have spoken to each other since their interview?' Dr Calvin asked.

'Quite sure,' Black said firmly.

'I'm going to be sitting in the chair in the centre,' Calvin told Kallner. 'I must see the tiniest movement.'

'Right.'

'Then let's try it one last time.'

She sat in the chair, silent, eyes restless. A heavy rock dropped downwards . . .

And a single robot stood up and took two steps forwards. And stopped.

Dr Calvin was up, too, her finger pointed at him. 'Nestor 10, come here,' she cried sharply. 'COME HERE!'

Slowly, unwillingly, the robot moved forwards.

'Get every other robot out of the room, Black,' the psychologist shouted, without taking her eyes from the robot. 'Get them out quickly, and keep them out.'

Nestor 10 came nearer. 'I was told to get lost – I must obey. I've been found – you're so weak and slow – I'm powerful and intelligent – they must not catch me – no-one must find me – no-one . . .'

Another step and a metal arm pushed Dr Calvin's shoulder. The arm was so heavy that Dr Calvin fell to the ground, with the arm across her body. It did not move.

And now faces were bending over her.

'Are you hurt?' Black asked anxiously.

She shook her head as they moved Nestor 10 and lifted her up. 'What happened?'

'I flooded the area with radiation,' Black explained. 'When we realized that he was attacking you, there was no time to do anything else. Just enough radiation to destroy Nestor 10, but not enough to harm you.'

'I don't think he was attacking, exactly,' said Dr Calvin weakly. 'He was *trying* to, but his changed First Law was still holding him back.'

*

Later, Calvin explained to Bogert and Kallner how she had tricked Nestor 10.

'We warned all the robots that there would be radiation between themselves and the human being. So they didn't move.'

'Yes, yes, I understand that. But why did Nestor 10 move?'

'That was an arrangement between Mr Black and myself. It wasn't dangerous radiation that flooded the area, but harmless light. Ordinary heat. Harmless. Nestor 10 knew that it was harmless and so he began to rush forwards. Then

*Dr Calvin fell to the ground, with the arm across her body.*

he realized that the normal NS-2s could sense radiation but couldn't recognize the different types of radiation. Nestor 10 could, because he had worked with Mr Black here and had learnt about the different types of radiation from him. To the normal robot, the area was fatal, because we told them that radiation was fatal. But Nestor 10 knew that we had lied. And for a moment he forgot that the other robots knew less than he did.'

# EVIDENCE

We finished our coffee and Dr Calvin began to talk about the developments of the last fifty years.

'Earth became too small for nations, and the change from nations to Regions was begun by robots. I'm thinking of a man who died last year.' Her voice was suddenly deeply sad. 'He arranged to die, because he knew that we needed him no longer. Stephen Byerley.'

'Yes, I guessed that you were talking about him.'

'He first entered government in 2032. You were only a boy then, so you won't remember his strange election as City Governor . . .'

*

Francis Quinn was a politician, and he came to see Alfred Lanning with a problem.

Quinn's voice was friendly. 'I think you know Stephen Byerley?'

Dr Lanning, sitting at the other side of the desk, frowned impatiently. 'I have heard of him. I believe he may be our next City Governor.'

'That's right. At the moment he's only a lawyer. But if enough people vote for him at the election, three months from now, he will become the next governor.'

Lanning was becoming impatient. 'Mr Quinn, I have no interest in politicians —'

'But this matter is important for US Robots. You will understand if I tell you one thing: Mr Byerley never eats!'

Lanning's eyes were sharp. 'I find that quite extraordinary!'

Francis Quinn's expression was amused. 'I have investigated Stephen Byerley carefully during the past year. His life has been quite ordinary: brought up in a small town, educated at university, a car accident, arrival in the city. And in this city, no one has ever seen him eat or drink. Never! And no one has seen him sleep.'

Lanning shook his head. 'You're trying to tell me one thing, and that one thing is impossible.'

'He's a robot, Dr Lanning.'

Lanning's old eyes were surprisingly sharp. 'That's impossible. You know that US Robots is the only company in the solar system which makes positronic brains, and the company has never made a robot with a human appearance and a human character.'

'However, your company will have to investigate this,' Quinn went on smoothly. 'You know very well that there are strict laws against the use of positronic robots on the planets. If Byerley *is* a robot, think of the trouble it will cause your company. Think of the public shock and horror . . .'

Lanning stared at him in cold anger, and waited for him to go on.

'What happens to the positronic brains of your robots when their working lives end?' Quinn asked with a pleasant smile.

'The positronic brains are either destroyed, or used for new robots,' Lanning explained, impatiently.

'But it would be possible for someone to get hold of one of those brains – unlawfully of course – and create a humanoid robot?'

'Scientifically, it would be possible to produce a humanoid robot, yes. But, Mr Quinn, it has not been done, I promise you!'

\*

Stephen Byerley was forty years old, and he looked forty years old. He looked healthy and pleasant, particularly when he laughed. And he was laughing now.

'Really, Dr Lanning – a robot? I – I – a robot?'

Lanning frowned and looked at Dr Calvin who was sitting next to him. She was silent.

'Someone has told us that you are a robot, and we must investigate because our company is the only producer of positronic brains,' Lanning explained coldly.

'Oh yes, your position is clear to me. I'm sorry if my laughter upset you. How can I help you?'

'Will you sit down in a restaurant, with witnesses present, and eat?' Lanning asked quietly.

Dr Calvin watched Byerley carefully, and he looked at her for a moment before turning back to Lanning. 'I don't think that I can do that. I know Francis Quinn, you see. He doesn't want me to become City Governor and so he's invented this story. It's nonsense. I don't sleep much and I don't eat in public. Is that what Quinn's reports say?' He turned to Dr Calvin. 'You're the company's psychologist?'

'Robot psychologist, please.'

'Right. Well, as a psychol – robot psychologist, I guess that you've brought some food with you this morning.'

An expression of surprise crossed Susan Calvin's face. She opened her bag and produced an apple which she handed silently to Byerley across his desk.

Calmly, Stephen Byerley bit into the apple and calmly, he swallowed it.

Dr Lanning smiled widely. But only for a second.

'I was curious to see if you would eat it,' Susan Calvin said. 'But of course, it proves nothing.'

'It doesn't?' Lanning asked.

'Of course not. It's obvious that if this man is a humanoid robot, he will be a perfect copy. Look at his skin, his eyes, the bones in his hand. If he's a robot, then I wish that US Robots had made him, because he's a good job. Whoever made him so perfectly would make sure that he could eat and sleep if necessary.'

'Now wait,' Lanning said angrily. 'I'm not interested in whether Mr Byerley is human or not. I'm only interested in protecting US Robots. A public meal will end the matter.'

'But you forget that I want to become governor,' Byerley said. 'If Quinn wants to call me a robot, then I will play the game with him.'

Lanning looked unhappy. 'He's going to say publicly that you are a robot.'

'Exactly. Let him tell everyone. I shall defeat him in the end, by using his own weapon against him.'

Susan Calvin rose to her feet. 'Come, Dr Lanning. He won't change his mind.'

'You see.' Byerley smiled gently. 'You're a human psychologist, too.'

*

Perhaps Byerley was not quite so confident that evening when he arrived home. The man in the wheelchair looked up and smiled.

'You're late, Steve,' he whispered. He opened his mouth with difficulty.

'I know, John,' Byerley said gently. 'A peculiar problem delayed me.'

John's face had obviously been terribly burned years ago, but his eyes were clear. They were anxious now. 'Nothing you can't solve?'

'I'm not exactly sure. I may need your help: you're the clever one in the family. Let's go out into the garden. It's a beautiful evening.'

Two strong arms lifted John from the wheelchair and gently Byerley carried him through the house into the garden. Carefully, he put John down on the grass.

'Tell me about your problem.'

'Quinn is going to fight me as governor. He's going to say publicly that I'm a robot.'

John's eyes opened wide. 'It's impossible. I don't believe it.'

'It's true. Two scientists from US Robots came to my office today to argue with me.'

John's thin hands pulled at the grass. 'I see.'

'But I've an idea. Listen to me and tell me if we can do it.'

*

Francis Quinn stared at Alfred Lanning. Lanning stared fiercely at Susan Calvin, who stared quietly at Quinn.

'We've done what you asked,' Lanning said for the second time. 'We've witnessed the man eat. He's not a robot.'

*Gently Byerley carried him through the house into the garden.*

At last, Quinn turned to Calvin. 'You've said nothing. Tell me what you think.'

'Now, Susan —' Lanning warned.

'Let her talk,' Quinn said smoothly.

Susan Calvin fixed cold eyes on Quinn. 'There are only two ways to prove Byerley is a robot. You can X-ray him. Or you can study his psychology. If he has a positronic brain, then he must obey the Three Laws of Robotics. Do you know them?'

Quinn nodded.

'If Byerley breaks any of those laws, then he isn't a robot. If he follows all the laws, he may be a robot. Or he may simply be a very good man.'

'So you're telling me that you can never prove him a robot?'

'I may be able to prove that he *isn't* a robot.'

The politician stood up. 'Then we shall see what Mr Byerley's body looks like under his skin. Somehow, I'm going to get evidence that he's a robot.' And he left the room.

Lanning turned impatiently to Calvin. 'Why do you insist on —'

'I won't lie for you,' she replied sharply.

'And what happens to US Robots if he opens up Byerley and a lot of wheels and electrical bits and pieces fall out? What then?'

'He won't open up Byerley,' said Calvin confidently. 'Byerley is at least as clever as Quinn.'

\*

The newspapers were full of reports about the robot

Byerley. Nobody could talk about anything else. At first there was loud laughter, but soon people began to wonder. What if it was true? The idea was terrifying, impossible! Nobody would vote for Byerley, if evidence was produced that he was a robot.

Those people who opposed the development of robots demanded new laws, and public anger began to grow. There were guards with guns around every US Robots office and factory, and police protection for Byerley day and night. Reporters and photographers waited outside Byerley's house, and interviewed scientists from US Robots. Soon, a city official with two policemen arrived to search Byerley's home.

Quietly, Byerley read the letter from one of the city judges. Then he nodded. 'Do your job.'

The official left the room with the two policemen to search the house. They were back in ten minutes.

'Mr Byerley, we want to search you. We've brought an X-ray machine.'

Byerley laughed and shook his head. 'You can't search me. I've read the description in the judge's letter of what you can search: my house, my garden, the garage and any other buildings in my garden. You can't search me.'

The men marched to the door. Then the official turned, his hand in his pocket. 'You're a clever lawyer,' he said angrily. For a moment, he stood there. Then he left, waved to the reporters outside the house, and shouted, 'We'll have something for you tomorrow.'

In his car, he removed a tiny machine from his pocket and carefully inspected it. It was the first time he had taken an

X-ray with the new machine. He hoped that he had done it correctly.

*

Quinn and Byerley had never met face to face. But the following day Quinn phoned Byerley on the videophone.

'I intend to tell the public that you're wearing special clothes which prevent X-ray photographs,' Quinn began. 'It's obvious that you don't dare face an X-ray.'

Byerley was friendly. 'I won't have an X-ray because I want to protect my private life. It's obvious that you don't care about anyone's private life – or about protecting people from unlawful behaviour. However, I do care, and voters might be interested in that difference between us.'

'A very interesting idea. But no one will believe you.' Quinn looked at the paper in his hand. 'Another thing: your friend isn't at your home.'

'My old teacher,' Byerley said calmly. 'He's in the country – has been for two months.'

'Your teacher? A scientist?'

'A lawyer, and a scientist, before his accident. His health is so poor that he can do little work now.'

Quinn was unsmiling. 'What does he know about robots?'

Byerley stared at Quinn's face on the video screen, but his expression did not change. 'I'm no judge of that.'

'Your teacher is the real Stephen Byerley. He created you. No one's going to vote for you. You're a robot.'

Byerley gave a wide smile. 'You won't be able to prove that. As for losing the election . . . well, a while ago I was an unknown lawyer. Now, thanks to you, I'm world-famous.'

*

Byerley's teacher came back to the city a week before the election.

'Your job went well?' Byerley asked.

'Well enough. There will be no trouble there.'

'There's some risk of violence in the city during the election, but I don't think it will be dangerous. Be sure to watch the television tomorrow, John.' And Byerley touched his hand gently.

*

The crowd was huge. Many people were angry, because they did not want a robot to be their new governor. From his platform, Byerley spoke slowly and calmly, but few listened. The screams and shouts from the angry crowd grew louder.

Then a tall, thin man pushed to the front of the crowd. 'Hit me!' he shouted.

'Quiet! Quiet!' shouted some people near him.

'Hit me!' the man said again. 'If you're not a robot, prove it. Hit me!' He climbed up on to the platform.

The crowd was silent now.

'I have no reason to hit you,' Byerley said clearly.

The thin man began to laugh wildly. 'You *can't* hit me. You *won't* hit me. You're not human. You're a machine – an ugly machine!'

And Stephen Byerley, in front of thousands in the crowd and in front of millions who were watching on television, lifted his arm and then hit the man hard on the chin. The man went over backwards with nothing on his face but surprise.

*Stephen Byerley hit the man hard on the chin.*

Dr Calvin, watching from a special seat in front, got up and walked away. One reporter ran after her.

Susan Calvin called over her shoulder, 'There's your evidence. He's human.'

*

Dr Calvin and Stephen Byerley met once again – a week before Byerley moved into the governor's house.

'I'm sorry that it ended like this,' the psychologist said. 'I like robots better than I like human beings. I'd like to see a robot governing the world. He'd be unable to harm human beings and so he'd govern better than any human being. Because of the Laws of Robotics, a robot could never be cruel, stupid or unjust. It would be the perfect answer to the problems of government.'

'Except that the positronic brain isn't as capable as the human brain.'

'He'd have advisers. Not even a human brain is capable of governing without advisers.'

Byerley considered Susan Calvin with interest. 'Why are you smiling, Dr Calvin?'

'Because Mr Quinn didn't think of everything. For three months before the election, your teacher was in the country for some mysterious reason. He returned just before that famous violence of yours. And after all, what he had done once, he could do a second time.'

'I don't quite understand.'

Dr Calvin rose. She was obviously ready to leave. 'I mean that there is one time when a robot may harm a human being without breaking the First Law.'

'And when is that?'

Dr Calvin was at the door. She said quietly, 'When the human being is another robot.'

And then she smiled widely, her thin face shining. 'Goodbye, Mr Byerley. I shall vote for you again, five years from now – as Regional Governor.'

The door closed behind her.

*

I stared at Dr Calvin with horror. 'Is that true?'

'All of it,' she said.

'The great Byerley was a robot?'

'Oh, we can never find out. He arranged for his body to be destroyed, so there will never be any proof. But I believe that he was.'

'Yes, but —'

'No buts! Byerley was a very good City Governor, and five years later he *did* become Regional Governor. And in 2044 he became the first World Governor!'

There was silence for a long moment and then Dr Calvin got up from her chair. 'And that is all,' she said. 'I saw it from the beginning, when the poor robots couldn't speak, to now, when robots are the only real hope for the safety of human beings. I will see no more. My life is over. *You* will see what comes next.'

*

I never saw Susan Calvin again. She died last month at the age of eighty-two.

# GLOSSARY

**admit**  to agree to the truth of something

**asteroid**  a very small planet

**atomic**  of or relating to the energy that is produced when atoms are broken

**bar** *(n)*  a long, narrow piece of metal

**battery**  a metal case which contains and supplies electricity

**beam** *(n)*  a line of light or heat

**brain**  the part of the body inside the head which controls thought, memory and feeling

**cable** *(n)*  a kind of 'rope', made of thin pieces of metal, which carries electricity

**carbon monoxide**  a poisonous gas

**cigar**  a type of large cigarette

**circuit**  a circular path of electricity

**conflict** *(n)*  a serious difference of opinions, wishes, duties, etc.

**converter**  a machine that converts (changes) something into something else

**cross** *(n)*  a sign like the letter X

**detonator**  a piece of equipment used to explode things

**dot** *(n)*  a small, round mark

**election**  when people vote to choose the people to govern them

**electron**  a tiny part of an atom

**energy**  sources of power (e.g. from the sun, or burning fuel) that make machines work

**evidence**  information that gives a strong reason for believing something

**flash** *(n)*  a sudden bright light

**flash** *(v)*  to give or produce a bright light for a very short time

**gravity**  the force that pulls things towards the centre of a planet

**Hi**  used as a greeting, instead of 'Hello'

**initiative**  the ability and imagination to realize what needs to be done, and to do it without help or advice

**insosuit**  a suit which keeps the body at a safe temperature

**liar**  a person who does not tell the truth

**Mars**  the planet fourth in order from the sun

**Master**  a man who controls people, animals or things

**mathematician**  a person who studies the science of numbers

**Mercury**  the planet nearest the sun

**mine** *(n)*  a place under the ground from where valuable stones or rocks are taken

**mine** *(v)*  to dig in the ground for valuable stones or rocks

**novel** *(n)*  an invented story, long enough to fill a complete book

**ore**  rock from which metal can be taken

**oxygen**  a gas in the air, necessary for life

**photocell**  something which makes electricity from sunlight

**photocell bank**  a group of photocells

**plain** *(adj)*  not pretty

**planet**  a large object in space (e.g. the Earth) which moves around a star (e.g. the sun)

**positronic brain**  a brain which works by using positive electrons

**protect**  to keep safe

**protection**  keeping someone or something safe, or being kept safe

**psychologist**  someone who studies how the mind works

**rabbit**  a small, greyish-brown animal with long ears, which lives in holes in the ground

**radiation**  the sending out of energy (heat, light, etc.) in the form of rays

**robot**  a machine that can do many of the things that people do

**robotics**  the study of making and using robots

**serial number**  a number given to individual things (e.g. pieces of equipment) in a series of the same things

**solar** *(adj)*  of or relating to the sun

**space**  the universe beyond the Earth, where all other planets and stars are

**spit** *(v)*  to make liquid come out of one's mouth, often with force

**stew** *(n)*  a dish of meat and vegetables cooked slowly together in water

**subsidiary**  connected to, but of less importance than something else

**tonne**  a measure of weight equal to 1000 kilograms

**vibration**  a small, shaking movement

**X-ray** *(n)*  a powerful beam which can photograph the inside of the human body

# I, Robot
SHORT STORIES

---

# ACTIVITIES

## Before Reading

1 Read the story introduction on the first page of the book, and the back cover. How much do you know now about these stories? Circle Y (yes) or N (no) for each sentence.

1 Human beings need air, water, and food in order to live. Y/N
2 Human beings spend half their lives asleep. Y/N
3 Science fiction sometimes gives us a picture of the future which later proves to be true. Y/N
4 In the 1940s, most people thought that robots could do many of the jobs done by human beings. Y/N
5 Human beings like working in weather that is too hot. Y/N
6 Factories today use robots because they are reliable. Y/N
7 Dr Susan Calvin studies the psychology of robots. Y/N
8 Powell and Donovan are engineers who work with robots. Y/N
9 The stories in this book are about some of the problems Dr Calvin has with Powell and Donovan. Y/N

2 Can you guess what the robots in these stories are like, and what they might do? Choose the ideas that you think are most likely.

1 They can talk, think, and make decisions.
2 They are dangerous because they often attack human beings.
3 They look and sound exactly like human beings.
4 They do difficult, dangerous jobs on other planets.
5 They protect human beings from danger.
6 Like humans, they can feel love and hate, jealousy and greed.

# *While Reading*

**Read *The Three Laws of Robotics* and *Dr Susan Calvin*. Then answer these questions.**

1 In what order should a robot do these three things: protect itself, protect human beings, obey orders?
2 What were Dr Calvin's views on robots?

**Read *Runaround*, and then explain the problem with Speedy in relation to the Three Laws of Robotics.**

1 Which law sent Speedy to the selenium pool in the first place?
2 Which law prevented Speedy from collecting the selenium?
3 Which law prevented Speedy from returning to the Station?
4 Which law came into effect when Powell put himself in danger?
5 When Donovan sent Speedy out the second time, how did he make sure that the same problem did not happen again?

**Read *Reason*. Who said these words, and to whom? What or who were they talking about?**

1 'There should be a better explanation.'
2 'A black material with tiny shining dots on it.'
3 'You are a very inefficient and short-lived piece of equipment.'
4 'From now on I serve the Master.'
5 'It could run directly into the path of our Earth beam.'
6 'He'll have to change his mind when he sees that.'
7 'What does it matter what he believes?'
8 'I hope it's good, or I won't allow it to touch the controls.'

**Read *Catch that Rabbit*, and then answer these questions.**

1  What did Powell mean by 'We've got to catch that rabbit'?
2  Why was there usually no need to speak to a subsidiary robot?
3  What did Dave need to use during emergencies more than during ordinary times?
4  Why did Powell and Donovan blow up part of the tunnel?
5  How were orders to the subsidiaries different in an emergency?
6  How did destroying one of the subsidiaries solve the problem?

**Read *Liar*. Then complete sentences 1 to 6 with the right parts of sentences below.**

1  Herbie knew that Dr Calvin loved Milton Ashe, . . .
2  Bogert wanted to be the next Managing Director, . . .
3  Herbie also knew what the mistake in the factory had been, . . .
4  Dr Calvin realized that Herbie had been telling lies . . .
5  She realized that Herbie couldn't tell people the truth . . .
6  Telling the truth would be a psychological injury, . . .

7  but he knew that Lanning and Bogert wanted to discover the mistake for themselves, . . .
8  but he couldn't tell her that Ashe didn't love her . . .
9  and so Herbie would be breaking the First Law, . . .
10  if he knew that the truth would hurt them, . . .
11  so Herbie told him that Dr Lanning had resigned . . .
12  when Ashe told her about the girl he planned to marry.
13  so he told them that he didn't know the answer.
14  which a robot can never do.
15  because that information would have hurt her.
16  so he had to give people the answers they wanted to hear.
17  although he knew that wasn't true.

Read *Little Lost Robot*. Here are some false sentences about the story. Change them into true sentences.

1  The brains of all NS-2s contained only part of the First Law.
2  The normal NS-2s allowed humans to go near the radiation.
3  In the test the robots moved forwards to save the man although they knew that the electric cable would kill them first.
4  The NS-2s which had just arrived knew all about radiation.
5  Bogert advised the robots to sit where they were unless they noticed any radiation between them and the human being.
6  The test involved harmful radiation from light and heat.
7  Nestor 10 was caught in the end because he remembered that the other robots knew more than he did about radiation.

Read *Evidence*. Choose the best question-word for these questions, and then answer them.

*How / What / Why*

1  . . . did Francis Quinn suspect Byerley of being a robot?
2  . . . happened to the positronic brains of the robots at US Robots when their working lives ended?
3  . . . did the business with the apple prove?
4  . . . would it prove if Byerley broke any of the Three Laws of Robotics?
5  . . . would it prove if he followed all Three Laws?
6  . . . didn't the secret X-ray provide any proof?
7  . . . did Byerley prove to the crowd that he was not a robot?
8  . . . would Dr Calvin like to see a robot governing the world?
9  . . . will nobody ever be sure if Byerley was a robot or not?
10  . . . did Dr Calvin believe that Byerley was a robot?

# After Reading

1 **When Greg Powell returned from Mercury, he wrote a report for Dr Calvin. Choose one suitable word to fill each gap.**

The photocell banks which protected us _____ the heat of Mercury's sun were _____. We needed selenium to repair them, _____ we sent Speedy to a selenium _____ to bring us some selenium. Hours _____, Speedy still hadn't returned, so we _____ to go after Speedy on the _____ from the First Expedition. They couldn't _____ without human control, so we rode _____ through the tunnels of the mining _____ to an exit which was five _____ from the selenium pool. We went _____ the station and stood in the _____ of a tall cliff, where the _____ was eighty centigrade. We saw Speedy _____ towards us, but when we called _____, he turned and ran away, singing.

_____ was obviously something confusing his brain _____. We thought that he was probably _____ some danger at the pool. The _____ Law sent him towards the pool, _____ then the Third Law drove him _____ again.

I decided to go out _____ the sun to see if Speedy _____ save me. I rode on the _____ robot towards the pool, and then _____ on foot. Ten minutes passed. I _____ Speedy on my radio. He stopped, _____ did not turn. I was now _____ with difficulty. I called him again. _____, I felt metal fingers on my _____. Speedy picked me up and carried _____ into the shadow of the cliff. _____ time, Donovan explained that the _____ was essential and sent him to _____ pool. He was back within forty-two _____.

2 **If Miller had been less unfriendly, perhaps Powell would have warned him about Cutie. Imagine he did, and complete their conversation. (Use as many words as you like.)**

MILLER: How's this new robot? I hope it's good!

POWELL: It *is* rather good. You won't _____.

MILLER: Why not?

POWELL: Well, the robot won't _____ because he believes that _____.

MILLER: Have you told him that *you* made him?

POWELL: Of course we have, but _____. Perhaps it doesn't matter. Last week an _____ and the robot _____.

MILLER: So what am I going to do with the robot while I'm on the station?

POWELL: _____.

3 **Put Powell's notes in the right order and then make a summary of the problems he and Donovan faced in *Catch that Rabbit*.**

1 create emergency / watch / roof fell in / trapped in tunnel / robots dancing

2 emergencies / all six subsidiaries / orders at same time / circuits overloaded / crazy orders

3 robot and six subsidiaries / worked well / a team / only when watched / not watched / no work

4 idea / destroyed one subsidiary / robot became normal / rescue

5 normal situations / routine jobs / orders given separately

6 robot / test / interview subsidiary / orders / emergency / dance or march

4 Imagine that Herbie (in *Liar!*) had told the truth to the four humans in the story. What would he have said? Give his replies to these questions.

  1 DR CALVIN: What does Milton Ashe really think about me? Are you sure he isn't in love with someone else?
    HERBIE: _____.

  2 MILTON ASHE: What's Dr Calvin's secret, Herbie? Why is she using perfume and smiling at me all the time?
    HERBIE: _____.

  3 DR LANNING: I'm a bit worried about Bogert. Does he think I'm a good Managing Director? Is he happy working for me?
    HERBIE: _____.

  4 PETER BOGERT: I'm the best mathematician around here, and I'll soon be giving the orders too. Isn't that right, Herbie?
    HERBIE: _____.

5 Gerald Black wrote a letter to a friend to tell him about the 'little lost robot'. Use the words below (one word for each gap) to complete his letter. Not all the words will be needed.

*annoyed, answer, attacked, careful, careless, destroyed, different, electricity, hid, imitated, obey, order, psychologist, psychology, radiation, realize, recognize, responsible, results, similar, solve, taught, tests, trick*

Dear Jim

Last week Susan Calvin, a robot _____, came up from Earth to _____ a problem we had here. I was partly _____ for it because I'd got _____ with a Nestor robot and told him to get lost! He took this as an _____ that he had to _____. He then _____ himself

96

among a group of _____ robots and either _____ what they did or
_____ them to do what he did, so Dr Calvin's _____ couldn't catch
him. She finally caught him by a _____. Nestor 10 could _____
different types of _____, but the other robots couldn't. In the last
test Nestor 10 forgot that, and then he _____ Dr Calvin and had to
be _____. In future I shall be more _____ what I say to robots!
Best wishes, Gerald

6 **This is a summary of *Evidence*. Put the sentences in the right order
and then join them to make a paragraph of six sentences. Use these
linking words, and change names to pronouns (*she*, *he*, *him*, etc.)
where appropriate. (Begin with 11.)**

*and / because / but / if / so / which / while*

1 Byerley was wearing special clothes.
2 No one had ever seen Byerley eat or drink.
3 Dr Calvin gave Byerley an apple, which he ate.
4 Byerley then hit the man hard on the chin.
5 A man came up to the platform and called Byerley an ugly
   machine.
6 This proved to the crowd that Byerley was human.
7 Byerley would not have been able to injure a human being.
8 Byerley was speaking to the crowd during the election.
9 The photographs did not show anything.
10 Later, an official took some X-ray photographs of Byerley.
11 Francis Quinn thought that Byerley was a robot.
12 Dr Calvin met Byerley.
13 Byerley had been a robot.

7 Perhaps this is what some of the characters in the stories were thinking. Which six characters were they (one from each story), and what was happening in the story at that moment?

1 'She's gone now. I can see into her mind, and I know that she loves him – but I can also see into his mind, and I know that he doesn't love her. How complicated it all is! But I had no choice – I couldn't tell her the truth, because I can't hurt her.'

2 'I must get away from the danger at the pool – I must get the selenium from the pool – I must . . . Who's that? Someone's calling me. There he is, walking towards me. It's too hot for him out here in the sun. I must go to him at once.'

3 'One of my subsidiaries is down! What's happened? I think there was an emergency in the tunnel. Ah, I can hear the boss calling me – and there's the light from his torch. I must leave my subsidiary and go and help him.'

4 'Nobody else will ever find out the truth – I'm sure of it. She knows, but she's a good psychologist, of course, so I'm not surprised. But she must be happy about it, because she says she'll vote for me again.'

5 'It's a complicated job, putting together a new robot. They work carefully and they're quite good at it, but their brains are probably too weak to understand the Truth about the Master.'

6 'They'll never find me because I'm cleverer than all of them! But I must talk to the other robots now. I shall tell them not to rush forwards because the electricity will kill us before we can save the human.'

8  Choose three possible titles for each story. One title in each group is better than the others. Can you explain why?

- One Subsidiary Too Many
- Truth Hurts
- Electron Storm
- The City Governor
- Gerald Black's Mistake
- The Selenium Pool
- Get Lost!
- Personal Initiative
- Dr Calvin's Secret

- Robot or Human?
- Mercury Sunside
- Trapped in the Tunnel
- Serving the Master
- Death by Slow Boiling
- Does He Eat?
- Mind-Reader
- Dangerous Radiation
- Who Created the Parts?

9  Which of these statements do you agree with (A), and which do you disagree with (D)? Explain why you think this.

1  A human being is an inefficient piece of equipment; a robot is a perfect and efficient machine.

2  Robots are the only real hope for the future of human beings.

3  Many jobs – such as driving buses or trains, rubbish collection, cleaning the streets, looking after children, doing housework – could be done better by robots than by human beings.

4  'I like robots better than I like human beings. I'd like to see a robot governing the world.'

5  Robots will never be able to do everything that human beings can do.

10  Do you enjoy watching science-fiction films or television programmes? Describe one that you have seen, and explain why you enjoyed it or did not enjoy it.

# ABOUT THE AUTHOR

Isaac Asimov was born in Russia near Smolensk in 1920. He was brought to the United States by his parents three years later, and grew up in Brooklyn. He graduated in chemistry from Columbia University, New York, and went on to study biochemistry, becoming an associate professor of biochemistry at Boston University School of Medicine in 1955. He became a full-time writer in 1958, but still kept his connections with the University. During a long and busy career he wrote a huge number of books, including many works of popular science, such as *The Human Brain* (1964) and *Asimov's Guide to Science* (1972). He died in 1992.

Asimov's greatest fame lies with his science-fiction writing. He was already reading science fiction by the time he was nine, and he published his first short story in a magazine before he was twenty. He went on to write hundreds of short stories and many novels, several of which have won awards. His best-known and most popular works are the *Foundation* series (1942–50) and the classic collection, *I, Robot* (1950), which made famous the 'three laws of robotics' and which contains many clever logical puzzles. More robot stories appeared in 1976 in *The Bicentennial Man and Other Stories*.

Asimov's writing is clear and uncomplicated, and pays close attention to scientific detail. His contribution to the genre of science fiction is enormous. His robot stories alone have shaped the way we think of mechanical men, and his story 'Nightfall', written in 1941, is still considered to be one of the best SF stories ever written.

# OXFORD BOOKWORMS LIBRARY

*Classics • Crime & Mystery • Factfiles • Fantasy & Horror*
*Human Interest • Playscripts • Thriller & Adventure*
*True Stories • World Stories*

The OXFORD BOOKWORMS LIBRARY provides enjoyable reading in English, with a wide range of classic and modern fiction, non-fiction, and plays. It includes original and adapted texts in seven carefully graded language stages, which take learners from beginner to advanced level. An overview is given on the next pages.

All Stage 1 titles are available as audio recordings, as well as over eighty other titles from Starter to Stage 6. All Starters and many titles at Stages 1 to 4 are specially recommended for younger learners. Every Bookworm is illustrated, and Starters and Factfiles have full-colour illustrations.

The OXFORD BOOKWORMS LIBRARY also offers extensive support. Each book contains an introduction to the story, notes about the author, a glossary, and activities. Additional resources include tests and worksheets, and answers for these and for the activities in the books. There is advice on running a class library, using audio recordings, and the many ways of using Oxford Bookworms in reading programmes. Resource materials are available on the website <www.oup.com/bookworms>.

The *Oxford Bookworms Collection* is a series for advanced learners. It consists of volumes of short stories by well-known authors, both classic and modern. Texts are not abridged or adapted in any way, but carefully selected to be accessible to the advanced student.

---

You can find details and a full list of titles in the *Oxford Bookworms Library Catalogue* and *Oxford English Language Teaching Catalogues*, and on the website <www.oup.com/bookworms>.

# THE OXFORD BOOKWORMS LIBRARY
## GRADING AND SAMPLE EXTRACTS

### STARTER • 250 HEADWORDS

present simple – present continuous – imperative –
*can/cannot, must* – *going to* (future) – simple gerunds …

Her phone is ringing – but where is it?

Sally gets out of bed and looks in her bag. No phone. She looks under the bed. No phone. Then she looks behind the door. There is her phone. Sally picks up her phone and answers it. *Sally's Phone*

### STAGE 1 • 400 HEADWORDS

… past simple – coordination with *and, but, or* –
subordination with *before, after, when, because, so* …

I knew him in Persia. He was a famous builder and I worked with him there. For a time I was his friend, but not for long. When he came to Paris, I came after him – I wanted to watch him. He was a very clever, very dangerous man. *The Phantom of the Opera*

### STAGE 2 • 700 HEADWORDS

… present perfect – *will* (future) – *(dont) have to, must not, could* –
comparison of adjectives – simple *if* clauses – past continuous –
tag questions – *ask/tell* + infinitive …

While I was writing these words in my diary, I decided what to do. I must try to escape. I shall try to get down the wall outside. The window is high above the ground, but I have to try. I shall take some of the gold with me – if I escape, perhaps it will be helpful later. *Dracula*

## STAGE 3 • 1000 HEADWORDS

*... should, may* – present perfect continuous – *used to* – past perfect –
causative – relative clauses – indirect statements ...

Of course, it was most important that no one should see
Colin, Mary, or Dickon entering the secret garden. So Colin
gave orders to the gardeners that they must all keep away
from that part of the garden in future. *The Secret Garden*

## STAGE 4 • 1400 HEADWORDS

... past perfect continuous – passive (simple forms) –
*would* conditional clauses – indirect questions –
relatives with *where/when* – gerunds after prepositions/phrases ...

I was glad. Now Hyde could not show his face to the world
again. If he did, every honest man in London would be proud
to report him to the police. *Dr Jekyll and Mr Hyde*

## STAGE 5 • 1800 HEADWORDS

... future continuous    future perfect –
passive (modals, continuous forms) –
*would have* conditional clauses – modals + perfect infinitive ...

If he had spoken Estella's name, I would have hit him. I was so
angry with him, and so depressed about my future, that I could
not eat the breakfast. Instead I went straight to the old house.
*Great Expectations*

## STAGE 6 • 2500 HEADWORDS

... passive (infinitives, gerunds) – advanced modal meanings –
clauses of concession, condition

When I stepped up to the piano, I was confident. It was as if I
knew that the prodigy side of me really did exist. And when I
started to play, I was so caught up in how lovely I looked that
I didn't worry how I would sound. *The Joy Luck Club*

# Do Androids Dream of Electric Sheep?

## PHILIP K. DICK

*Retold by Andy Hopkins and Joc Potter*

San Francisco lies under a cloud of radioactive dust. People live in half-deserted apartment buildings, and keep electric animals as pets because so many real animals have died. Most people emigrate to Mars – unless they have a job to do on Earth.

Like Rick Deckard – android killer for the police and owner of an electric sheep. This week he has to find, identify, and kill six androids which have escaped from Mars. They're machines, but they look and sound and think like humans – clever, dangerous humans. They will be hard to kill.

The film *Bladerunner* was based on this famous novel.

# The Dead of Jericho

## COLIN DEXTER

*Retold by Clare West*

Chief Inspector Morse is drinking a pint of beer. He is thinking about an attractive woman who lives not far away.

The woman he is thinking of is hanging, dead, from the ceiling of her kitchen. On the floor lies a chair, almost two metres away from the woman's feet.

Chief Inspector Morse finishes his pint, and orders another. Perhaps he will visit Anne, after all. But he is in no particular hurry.

Meanwhile, Anne is still hanging in her kitchen, waiting for the police to come and cut her down. She is in no hurry, either.